The Gingerbread Man
AND OTHER TALES

SCHOLASTIC INC.

New York   Toronto   London   Auckland   Sydney
Mexico City   New Delhi   Hong Kong   Buenos Aires

The Gingerbread Man, ISBN 0-590-41056-3
Text copyright © 1967 by Scholastic Inc.
Illustrations copyright © 1985 by Karen Schmidt.
Art direction by Diana Hrisinko. Book design by Emmeline Hsi.

Jack and the Beanstalk, ISBN 0-590-40164-5
Text copyright © 1965 by Scholastic Books, Inc.
Illustrations copyright © 1986 by Matt Faulkner.
Art direction/design by Diana Hrisinko.

The Three Billy-Goats Gruff, ISBN 0-590-41121-7
Illustrations copyright © 1984 by Ellen Appleby.

The Little Red Hen, ISBN 0-590-41145-4
Text copyright © 1985 by Scholastic Inc.
Illustrations copyright © 1985 by Lucinda McQueen.
Art direction by Diana Hrisinko. Book design by Emmeline Hsi.

12 11 10 9 8 7 6 5 4 3 2   5 6 7 8 9/0

Printed in the U.S.A.   24
This edition created exclusively for Barnes & Noble, Inc.
2004 Barnes & Noble Books
ISBN 0-7607-5801-8
First compilation printing, September 2004

The Gingerbread Man

AND OTHER TALES

The Gingerbread Man

Pictures by KAREN LEE SCHMIDT

Once upon a time there was
an old man
and an old woman
and a little boy.

One day the old woman said to the little boy,
"I will bake you a gingerbread man."
And she did.

The old woman put the gingerbread man into the pan.
And she put the pan into the oven.

"Now watch the oven,"
said the old woman. "And when you
can smell the gingerbread, call me.

But do NOT open the oven door."

Then the old woman
went to work in the garden
with the old man.

The little boy sat in the kitchen
and watched the oven.
Soon he could smell the gingerbread.

"I want to see if the gingerbread man
looks as good as he smells,"
said the little boy.

And he opened the
oven door.

The gingerbread man hopped out of the pan.
He hopped out of the oven.
He ran across the kitchen
to the open door.
The little boy ran to shut the door,
but the gingerbread man ran faster.

He ran
out of the
door and down
the steps and
into the road.

Then he called out,
  "Run, run
    as fast as you can.
    You can't catch me.
    I'm the gingerbread man."

The little boy ran after him.

The old man and the old woman
saw the gingerbread man. And they ran too.
But the gingerbread man ran faster.

And the little boy and the old man
and the old woman had to sit down to rest.

The gingerbread man ran on.
Soon he came to some farmers.

"Where are you going?"
shouted the farmers.

"I have run away from
a little boy
and an old man
and an old woman.
And I can run away from you too,"
said the gingerbread man.

"Oh you can, can you?" said the farmers.
And they dropped their rakes
and ran after him.

Then the gingerbread man called out,
 "Run, run
   as fast as you can.
   You can't catch me.
   I'm the gingerbread man."

The farmers ran fast.
But the gingerbread man ran faster.

And the farmers had to sit down to rest.

The gingerbread man ran on.
Soon he came to a bear.

"Where are you going?" shouted the bear.

"I have run away from
   a little boy
   and an old man
   and an old woman
   and three farmers.
   And I can run away from you too,"
   said the gingerbread man.

"Oh you can, can you?" the bear said.
And he began to run after the gingerbread man.
Then the gingerbread man called out,
   "Run, run
      as fast as you can.
   You can't catch me.
   I'm the gingerbread man."

The bear ran fast.
But the gingerbread man ran faster.

And the bear had to sit down to rest.

The gingerbread man ran on.
Soon he came to a wolf.

"Where are you going?" shouted the wolf.

"I have run away from
a little boy
and an old man
and an old woman
and three farmers
and a bear.
And I can run away from you too,"
said the gingerbread man.

"Oh you can, can you?" said the wolf.
And he began to run after the gingerbread man.

Then the gingerbread man called out,
"Run, run
as fast as you can.
You can't catch me.
I'm the gingerbread man."

The wolf ran fast.
But the gingerbread man ran faster.

And the wolf had to sit down to rest.

The gingerbread man ran on.
Soon he came to a fox.

The fox said,
"Where are you going?"

"I have run away from
a little boy
and an old man
and an old woman
and three farmers
and a bear
and a wolf.
And I can run away from you too,"
said the gingerbread man.

The fox said,
"I can't hear you,
gingerbread man.
Come a little closer."

The gingerbread man
stopped running.
He came a little closer
to the fox.

Then he called out,
"I have run away from
   a little boy
   and an old man
   and an old woman
   and three farmers
   and a bear
   and a wolf.
And I can run away from
   you too."

"I can't hear you," said the fox.
"Come a little closer."

The gingerbread man came very close to the fox.
Then he shouted, "I have run away from
a little boy
and an old man
and an old woman
and three farmers
and a bear
and a wolf.
And I can run away from
you too."

"Oh you can, can you?"
said the fox.

And snip-snap —
He opened his mouth. And he closed his mouth.

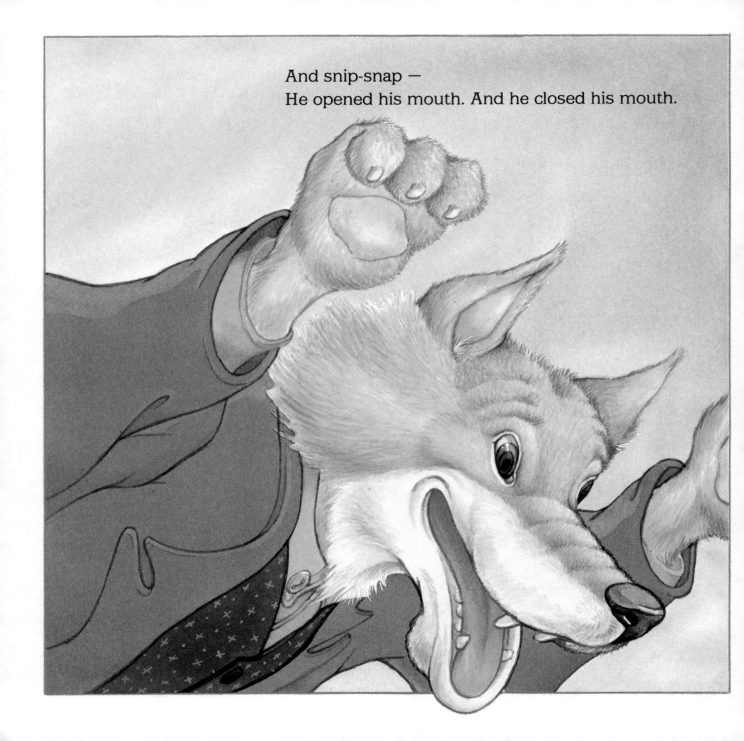

And that was the end of the gingerbread man!

Jack and the Beanstalk

Illustrated by MATT FAULKNER

In memory of
Tiki, Duke and Maggie
—M.F.

ONCE UPON A TIME
there was a poor old woman.
She had a son named Jack.

She had a cow named Milky White.
But that was all she had.

Every day the cow gave milk. And every day the old woman said to Jack, "Sell the milk and bring home the money." And he did. And that was all the money they had.

One morning the cow did not give milk.
"We must sell the cow," said Jack.
"Then take the cow," said the old woman, "and bring home some money."
So Jack took Milky White, and off they went.

Soon they met an old man.

"Good morning," said the old man. "That is a fine cow you have. Do you want to sell her?"

"Yes," said Jack. "Do you want to buy her?"

"Yes," said the old man.

"How much money will you give me?" said Jack.

"I have something better than money," said the old man.

"What is better than money?" said Jack.

"Look," said the old man.

"Beans!" said Jack.

"Yes," said the old man. "Give me your cow, and I will give you five beans."

"I don't want your beans," said Jack.

"But these beans are magic beans," said the old man. "Put them in the ground. Tomorrow they will grow up to the sky."

"Will they?" said Jack.

"They will," said the old man. "If they don't, I will give your cow back to you."

So the man took the cow. And Jack took the beans. He ran all the way home.

"Mother, Mother! See what I got for the cow!" said Jack.

"Good!" said his mother. "Give me the money."

Jack showed her the beans.

"Beans!" said his mother.

"They are magic beans," said Jack.

"Did you sell our cow for five beans? You fool!" said his mother.

"Take that! Take that! Take that!"

Then she took the beans and threw them out of the window.

Jack went to bed without any supper.
So did his mother. There was no money.
There was nothing to eat.

Poor Mother! Jack thought.
Poor me!
At last he fell asleep.

When Jack woke up, the room looked funny.
The sun was shining in one window.
But the other window was full of green leaves.

Jack ran to the window. And what do you
think he saw?

He saw a big beanstalk. The beanstalk
went up and up and up.
It went right up to the sky!

"They ARE magic beans!" said Jack.
"And this is a magic beanstalk."
He jumped onto the beanstalk.

And he climbed
and
he climbed
and he climbed
and he climbed.

At last he came to the sky. He saw a long road. The road went on and on and on. So Jack walked and walked and walked.

He came to a great big tall house. In front of the house
was a great big tall woman.

"Good morning," said Jack. "Please, can you give me some breakfast?"

"So you would like to eat breakfast," said the woman.

"Well, I know someone who would like to eat YOU for breakfast," she said. "My man is a giant. He likes to eat fresh boys on toast. And I hear him coming right now."

Thump. Thump. Thump.

"Please hide me," said Jack.

The woman was sorry for Jack. So she said, "Quick! jump in here."

And Jack jumped into the oven – just in time.
In came the giant.

"Ah! what's this I smell?" he said.
"Fee fi fo fum
I smell the blood of an Englishman.
Be he alive or be he dead,
I'll grind his bones to make my bread."
"Oh no, dear," said the giant's wife. "I think you can still smell the little boy you ate yesterday. Now don't be silly. Sit down and eat your breakfast."

Jack looked through a crack in the oven door.
He watched the giant.

The giant ate his breakfast. Then he took out two bags of gold and began to count the gold.

At last the giant began to get sleepy. His head began to nod. And he began to snore. He snored so loud, the house began to shake.

Then Jack jumped out of the oven.

He grabbed a bag of gold, and he ran and he ran until he came to the beanstalk.

The bag of gold was so heavy, Jack let it fall.
It fell down
   down
     down
into his mother's garden.

Then Jack climbed down
and climbed down.
And at last he was home.

"Mother! Mother!" Jack called. "Look at this!"
And he showed her the bag full of gold.
For a long time Jack and his mother
had plenty of money.

But one day all the money was gone. "Well," said Jack to his mother. "I will try my luck again."

So he got onto the beanstalk, and he climbed and
he climbed and he climbed
 and he climbed.
 At last he came to the road again.

And he found the great big tall house again. And in front of the house was the great big tall woman again.

"Good morning," said Jack, bold as brass. "Please, can you give me some breakfast?"

"You're the same boy who came here before!" said the great big tall woman.

"Maybe you can tell me what happened to the bag of gold the giant lost that day."

"Maybe I can," said Jack. "But I am so hungry, I can't talk."

"Then I'll give you something to eat," said the woman.

All at once —
thump thump thump.
They heard the giant coming.
   The woman hid Jack in the
oven. And everything happened
as it did before.
   The giant said, "Fee fi fo fum."
   His wife said, "Don't be silly."
   The giant ate his breakfast.

After breakfast, he said,
"Wife, bring the hen that lays
the golden eggs."
Then the giant said to the hen,
"Lay." And the hen laid
an egg all of gold.

At last the giant began to get sleepy.
His head began to nod.
And he began to snore.
He snored so loud,
the house began to shake.

Jack jumped out of the oven. He grabbed the hen and off he ran. But the hen made a noise, and the giant woke up.

Jack heard the giant call, "Wife, wife, what did you do with my golden hen?"

But that was all Jack heard. He ran to the beanstalk and climbed down like a house-on-fire.

"Mother! Mother!" Jack called.
"Look at this."
    Jack showed his mother the hen.

    "Lay," said Jack.
    The hen laid an egg all of gold.
    Every time Jack said, "Lay,"
the hen laid
a golden egg.

One day Jack said to his mother,
"Maybe the giant has more things.
I am going to try my luck again."
Jack got onto the beanstalk
and he climbed
and he climbed
and he climbed
and he climbed.

At last he got to the top.

But this time Jack did not go right to the giant's door.
This time he hid behind a bush. He saw the giant's wife
go down the road to get some water.
Jack crept into the house and
climbed into a big pot.

Soon he heard thump thump thump. The giant and his wife came in.
"Fee fi fo fum
I smell the blood of an Englishman," the giant said.
"Do you, my dear?" said the giant's wife. "Well, if it is that rascal Jack you smell, he will be in the oven. That is where he likes to hide."

They both ran to the oven.
The giant opened the door.
But Jack wasn't there,
thank goodness!

"Oh," said the giant's wife, "there you go again! I think you must be smelling the little boy you ate yesterday."

"Now don't be silly. Eat your breakfast."

The giant sat down to eat. He kept jumping up to look for Jack. But he did not look in the big pot, thank goodness!

After breakfast, the giant said, "Wife, bring me my golden harp."

She brought the harp and put it on the table.
"Sing," said the giant.
And the golden harp sang.
At last the giant began to get sleepy.
His head began to nod.
And he began to snore.
He snored so loud, the
house began to shake.

Then Jack crept out of the pot. He was as
quiet as a mouse. He crept to the table.
He climbed up the table leg.
He grabbed the harp. Then he
climbed down and began to run.

But the harp called out, "Master! Master!"
The giant woke up.
He was just in time to see Jack running off with his harp.

Jack ran as fast as he could. The giant came running after him.

Then Jack got onto the beanstalk and began to climb

down

down

down.

The giant stopped. He was afraid to climb down the beanstalk.

But the harp cried out once more, "Master! Master!"

So the giant jumped onto the beanstalk. He began
climbing down faster and faster.
But Jack was ahead of him.
"Mother! Mother!" Jack called.
"Bring me the ax! Bring me the ax!"

Jack's mother came running
with the ax.
She saw the giant's big feet.
She was so frightened,
she could not move.

But Jack jumped down.
He grabbed the ax.
He gave a chop at
the beanstalk.

The giant felt the beanstalk shaking.
Then Jack gave another chop with the ax.
The beanstalk fell to the ground,
and the giant fell with it.
And that was the end of the giant.

Then Jack showed his mother
the golden harp.

People paid money to hear the harp sing. And
every day the hen laid a golden egg.
So Jack and his mother became very rich.
And they lived happily ever after.

The Three Billy-Goats Gruff

A NORWEGIAN FOLKTALE

Illustrated by ELLEN APPLEBY

Once upon a time there were three billy-goats,
who were to go up to the hillside
to make themselves fat.

And the name of all three was "Gruff."

On the way up was a bridge.

And under the bridge lived a great ugly Troll,
with eyes as big as saucers
and a nose as long as a poker.

So first of all
came the youngest billy-goat Gruff
to cross the bridge.
TRIP, TRAP! TRIP, TRAP! went the bridge.

"WHO'S THAT tripping over my bridge?"
roared the Troll.

"Oh, it is only I,
    the tiniest billy-goat Gruff.

"I'm going up to the hillside
    to make myself fat,"
    said the billy-goat.

"Now I'm coming to gobble you up," said the Troll.

"Oh no! Please don't take me. I'm too little, that I am," said the billy-goat. "Wait for the second billy-goat Gruff. He's much bigger."

"Well, be off with you!" said the Troll.

A little while after came
the second billy-goat Gruff
to cross the bridge.

TRIP, TRAP! TRIP, TRAP! TRIP, TRAP! went the bridge.
"WHO'S THAT tripping over my bridge?" roared the Troll.

"Oh, it's the second billy-goat Gruff.
I'm going up to the hillside to make myself fat,"
said the billy-goat. And his voice was not so small.

"Now I'm coming to gobble you up," said the Troll.

"Oh no! Don't take me. Wait for the third billy-goat Gruff. He's much bigger."

"Very well, be off with you!" said the Troll.

But just then up came
the big billy-goat Gruff.

TRIP, TRAP! TRIP, TRAP! TRIP, TRAP!
went the bridge.

"WHO'S THAT tramping over my bridge?" roared the Troll.

"IT'S I! THE BIG BILLY-GOAT GRUFF," said the billy-goat.
And he had a very loud voice of his own.

"Now I'm coming to gobble you up," roared the Troll.

"Well, come along! I've got two spears,
And I'll poke your eyeballs out at your ears.
I've got besides two great, flat stones,
And I'll crush you to bits, body and bones."

That was what the big billy-goat said.

And that was what the big billy-goat did.

And after that he went up to the hillside.
There the billy-goats got so fat
they could hardly walk home again.
And if the fat hasn't fallen off them,
why, they're still fat. And so —

Snip, snap, snout,
This tale's told out.

The Little Red Hen

Pictures by LUCINDA McQUEEN

Once upon a time
there was a little red hen
who shared her tiny cottage with
a goose, a cat, and a dog.

The goose was a gossip.
She chatted with the neighbors
all day long.

The cat was very vain.

She brushed her fur,

straightened her whiskers,

and polished her claws
all day long.

The dog was always sleepy.

He napped on the front porch swing
all day long.

The Little Red Hen
ended up doing
all of the work
around the house.

She cooked.
She cleaned.

She washed the clothes

and took out the trash.

She mowed the lawn
and raked the leaves.
She even did all of
the shopping.

One morning on her way to market,
the Little Red Hen found
a few grains of wheat.
She put them in the pocket
of her apron.

When she got home
she asked her friends,
"Who will plant these grains
of wheat?"

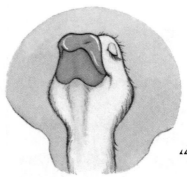

"Not I," said the goose.

"Not I," said the cat.

"Not I," said the dog.

"Then I will plant them myself,"
said the Little Red Hen.
And she did.

When the grains of wheat
began to sprout,
the Little Red Hen cried,
"Look, the wheat I planted is coming up!
Who will help me take care of it this summer?"

"Not I," said the goose.
"Not I," said the cat.
"Not I," said the dog.

"Then I will take care of it myself,"
said the Little Red Hen.
And she did.
All summer long she cared for the
growing wheat.
She made sure that it got enough water,
and she hoed the weeds out
carefully between each row.

By the end of summer
the wheat had grown tall.
And when it turned from green to gold,
she asked her friends,
"Who will help me cut
and thresh this wheat?"

"Not I," said the goose.
"Not I," said the cat.
"Not I," said the dog.

"Then I will cut and thresh it myself,"
    said the Little Red Hen.
    And she did.

When all of the wheat
had been cut and threshed,
the Little Red Hen scooped the wheat
into a wheelbarrow and said,
"This wheat must be ground into flour.
Who will help me take it to the mill?"

"Not I," said the goose.
"Not I," said the cat.
"Not I," said the dog.

"Then I will take it myself,"
said the Little Red Hen.
And she did.

The miller ground the wheat into flour
and put it into a bag for the Little Red Hen.

Then, all by herself,
she pushed the bag home
in the wheelbarrow.

One cool fall morning
not many days later,
the Little Red Hen got up early and said,
"Today would be a perfect day
to bake some bread.
Who will help me bake a loaf of bread
with the flour I brought home from the mill?"

"Not I," said the goose.   "Not I," said the cat.

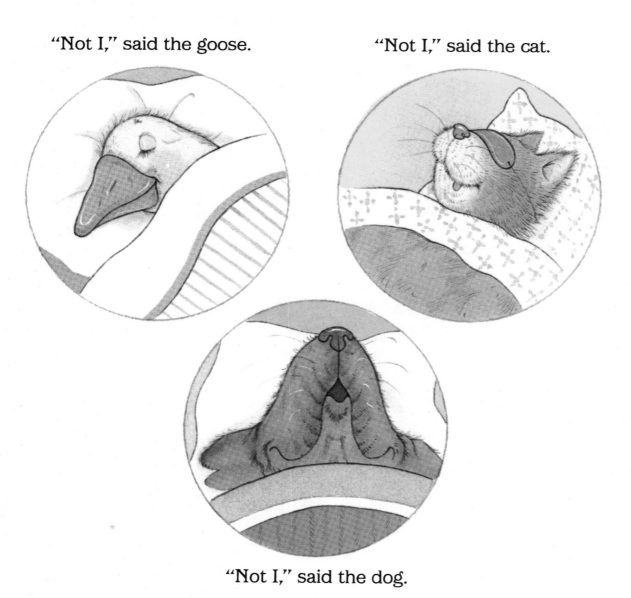

"Not I," said the dog.

"Then I will bake the bread myself,"
said the Little Red Hen.
And she did.

She mixed the flour with milk
and eggs and butter and salt.

She kneaded the dough

and shaped it into a nice plump loaf.

Then she put the loaf in the oven
and watched it as it baked.

The smell of the baking bread
soon filled the air.
It smelled so delicious
that the goose stopped chatting...
the cat stopped brushing...

...and the dog stopped napping.

One by one they came into the kitchen.

When the Little Red Hen
took the freshly baked loaf of bread
out of the oven, she said,
"Who will help me eat this bread?"

"Oh, I will!" said the goose.
"And I will!" said the cat.
"And I will!" said the dog.

"You will?" said the Little Red Hen.
"Who planted the wheat and took care of it?
  I did.

Who cut the wheat?

Who threshed it and took it to the mill?
I did.